COW

Makes a Difference

For Veronica

Cow Makes a Difference

Copyright © 2001 Baker Book House Company

New Kids Media™ is published by Baker Book House Company, P.O. Box 6287, Grand Rapids, MI 49516-6287

ISBN 0-8010-4475-8

Printed in China

2 3 4 5 6 7 – 03 02

Cow
Makes a Difference

 Todd Aaron Smith

NEW Kids MEDiA ®

 BAKER
A DIVISION OF
Baker Book House Co

Cow had some big ideas floating around in her little cow mind. She had been standing over by the fence post for a long time, just looking out across the field.

The farmer, who had been passing by, gave Cow a big smile and slowly said, "Now, don't you go getting any ideas about running off! Your place is right here on the farm!" And with that, he patted Cow on the back of her neck and quietly walked away.

Pig had walked up behind
the farmer and was now
standing at the fence
with Cow.
"Hello Cow!" Pig said.
"What's wrong? Is something
bothering you?"

Cow said, "I want to do something that will make people happy! I don't want to just stand around all the time! I want to make something of myself and make a difference!"

"HAHAHAHA!!! Have you lost your mind?" Pig said, laughing. You're nothing but a cow! HAHAHA!! You just keep on dreaming!"

As Pig walked off laughing, Cow quietly said to herself, "I'll show him! I'll show them all that I can be more than just a farm animal! Why, I'll even . . ."

Just then, in midsentence, a paper blew across the ground and stuck to Cow's leg. It was crumpled and wrinkled and dirty, and it had slowly drifted across the big open field, right over to Cow. She picked it up to see what it was.

Cow turned her head and looked off to the right. She noticed the city skyline. She stood looking wide-eyed at the big city. The paper had given Cow an idea.

Cow waited until it was dark. All the animals were asleep in their places. So was the farmer. Everything was quiet. Cow silently crept out of the barn and across the field. She let the gate shut behind her and crossed the wide open field of grass toward the big city lights.

By the next morning Cow had made it all the way to the big city.
She had finally arrived at the city zoo.

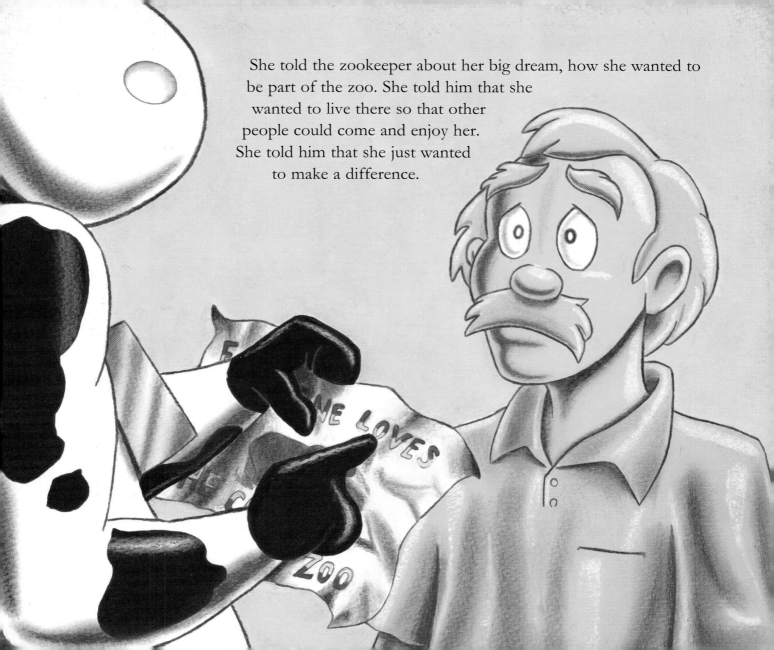

She told the zookeeper about her big dream, how she wanted to be part of the zoo. She told him that she wanted to live there so that other people could come and enjoy her. She told him that she just wanted to make a difference.

After a few moments of silence, the zookeeper tilted his head back and laughed. Finally, after he had mostly stopped laughing, he said, "You're a cow! People don't come to the zoo to see cows!"

The zookeeper continued, "People come to see tigers and elephants and lions and giraffes! You're just a common animal, like a dog and a cat! You don't see any dogs or cats at the zoo . . . right? I'm sorry . . . hahahaha . . . we just don't have any place for a cow!"

Cow left, disappointed by the zookeeper's words, but now more determined than ever! She began to wonder to herself, "What if I were a monkey? Would they welcome me into the zoo if I were a monkey?" She decided to find out.

It took a while, but Cow finally figured out how to dress up like a monkey.
Then, Cow was invited to live with the monkeys.

Cow had a great time playing with the monkeys, until finally she realized that it was nap time. She shut her eyes, but before she could go to sleep, she heard the sounds of the monkeys jumping, crashing, playing, and making cute monkey noises.

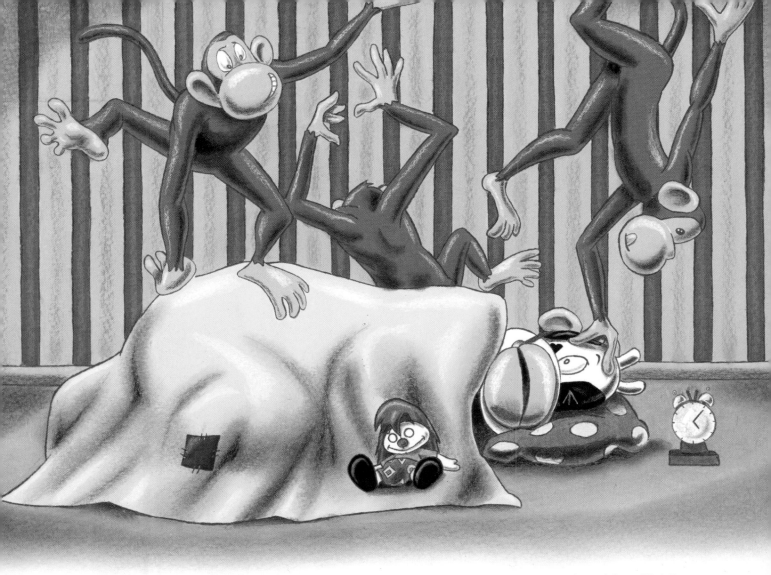

Cow tried very hard to sleep, but these monkeys wanted to jump around and be silly! It didn't take her very long to discover that cows do not make very good monkeys.

So, Cow dressed up to
look like the penguins
and moved in with them.
The penguins were very
cute, and Cow loved to
watch them waddle
around and swim in
the water.

Cow quickly realized, though, that it is very, very, very cold where the penguins live. Suddenly a penguin jumped into the water right next to Cow and Cow was splashed with freezing water. It took only a very short period of time to realize that cows do not make very good penguins.

Cow remembered that she had seen the lions lying around in the sun all day.
She decided to dress up like a lion and go and live with them.

After a short time of living with the lions, Cow discovered how loud and frightening the lions were. The lions were big and strong and Cow was very intimidated! She could see why cows do not make very good lions.

Cow was disappointed. She had tried her best to be a part of the zoo, but nothing really had worked for her. She just was not going to be very good at being any animal besides a cow.

Cow reluctantly decided to leave the zoo. God had made her a cow, and that's what she should be. She began thinking about the farm that she had left behind. No matter how badly she would like to be in the zoo, she could not be something that God did not create her to be.

"Hey, Cow!" called out the zookeeper's voice, "I heard about what you have been up to! I know that you dressed up like other animals so that you could be a part of the zoo! If you still want to be a part of the zoo, I will let you be in the children's petting zoo."

The zookeeper led her out into the petting zoo area, and several children came up to see her. Living in the big city, they had never seen a cow up close before! They hugged Cow and petted her! Everyone was so happy! Cow was especially happy!

Finally she was making a difference to someone, and all she had to do was be herself! This is what she really had always wanted! Cow thanked God for making her a cow.

Back at the farm the pigs were lying around in the mud. One pig eventually said, "I wonder what ever happened to that spotted cow that used to stand over there by the fence all day and daydream!" Just then a paper blew across the ground and stuck to the side of the fence . . .